THE HUMMINGBIRD & ANNIE, AND THEIR SPECIAL ABILITIES

Tatiana Tarnovaliysla

Somewhere, deep inside the Amazon rainforest, on the highest branches of a tall tree lived a family of two small, very con-spicuously-colored birds, in a nest which they had built themselves. They were the Hummingbirds, the most beautiful birds in the rainforest.

The Hummingbird family had two small white eggs in their nest; they would become parents soon. Every day, their main activity was to keep warm the eggs, until they hatched.

One day, the pair of birds flew down, close by, for lunch. They were looking for colorful, juicy, tropical flowers. All hummingbirds have a long, needle-like beak, which allows them to reach into the flowers for nectar, their favorite food.

While the Humming-
birds were busy finding food, a bad
bird, named Cuckoo, passed over the
tree and saw their nest. Cuckoo was
a famous egg thief across the Amazon rainforest. Cuckoo noticed the
two small eggs in the cozy Hummingbird nest. He looked around carefully
to ensure that nobody was watching.
Then, he picked up and hid one of the
small hummingbird eggs in his beak
quickly, with the mastery of a thief.
Then he flew away immediately, flee-
ing from the Amazon rainforest.

As the bad Cuckoo bird was fly-
ing, he approached a farm which was
owned by an old couple. It was full of

animals. Cuckoo landed on the fence, where Mama Chicken was having discussion with the cat.

"Hello Mama Chicken, can you come closer, please? I have something for you." Cuckoo said with some difficulty, as he still had the small egg in his beak.

The white Mama Chicken moved closer to the fence, towards Cuckoo "How can I help you, Cuckoo?"

"I have an offer for you Mama Chicken. I have brought you an exotic egg from the rainforest. I will give it to you, but in return you must give me some of the food that your human owners feed you. It is my favorite," Cuckoo said, without any shame.

"What have you done, Cuckoo?! Did you steal the egg?" the thought upset Mama Chicken "Bring it here, immediately!" Mama Chicken wanted to save the small unhatched egg from the irresponsible thief. Cuckoo jumped down and spat the small egg carefully on the soft grass.

"If you need a portion of food you could always come and ask for it, Cuckoo. We will never refuse you a meal. But now, you have stolen an egg from its family. You don't deserve any food. Leave our farm immediately, before I call my husband," Mama Chicken said, and Cuckoo left without the egg and without a meal.

Mama Chicken took the small egg and took it to her husband, Mr. Cocko, "Look, husband, the Cuckoo bird brought this small egg from the rainforest. What are we going to do with it now?"

"Well, Mama Chicken, we can't go to

the rainforest, it is too dangerous and too far away. We also can't abandon it. We will adopt it. If you agree, we will put the small egg in our nest with the rest of our unhatched eggs. We will raise it as one of our own, together with the rest of our chicks."

"Yes, Cocko, I agree, we need to take care of this egg," Mama Chicken took the small egg and placed it next to the other unhatched eggs in their warm nest.

After a few weeks, all the eggs hatched. Beautiful yellow chicks jumped from the warm nest with curiosity and excitement. The small jungle egg hatched too. It was a very small bird, and it hatched blind and without any plumage. It opened its

beak all the time, like it was trying to talk, but no one could hear its
voice. It seemed like it might be mute.
Mama Chicken took special care of
the baby bird: she kept it warm and
protected at all times. The small bird
couldn't eat the farm food independ-
ently, as its sisters and brothers did,
so Mama Chicken fed it with her beak.
After a few weeks, the small baby bird
opened its eyes. It wasn't blind; it just
needed some time to grow and be able
to see, but it couldn't be heard, even
when it tried very hard to talk to the
others. It also grew plumage, with
wonderfully colorful feathers. All the
animals in the farm visited Mama
Chicken's nest to admire the beauty
of the small chick. They all tried to

guess what kind of chicken it could be, as no one from the farm had seen that kind of colored plumage before.

Although the small bird had different colored plumage and couldn't be heard, even when it tried very hard to speak to them, none the members of the Chicken family or the other animals living in the farm treated him as a different bird. They treated it as an equal to its sisters and brothers. For them, it was just the small colorful chick. It was never discriminated against or excluded from the activities of the Chicken family.

One day, while playing with its brothers and sisters, the colorful chick discovered that it had a special talent: it could jump higher than the other chicks, while it fluttering its wings. It then started to jump from the ground to the fence, having fun and entertaining the rest of the chicks at the same time.

The colorful chick also liked singing, and had a very artistic nature. Even though no one could hear its voice, the colorful chick decided to do some repetitions. It had hope that its voice would be heard one day. One day, while the family was out on their regular walk, the small colorful chick jumped on the fence, took up a position like a real singer a stage. However, while it sang, it realized once again that nobody could hear it. Its voice was so high pitched that even when it screamed or sang as loud as an opera singer, nobody could hear its voice.

This made the colorful chick sad. It jumped onto a tree branch to be alone for a while. The farm dog, Mr. Doggy, approached the tree "Why are you sad, little chick?"

"Mr. Doggy, I am trying to sing for my family, but even though I have a voice, they can't hear me. Why am I even talking to you? Nobody can hear my voice," the colorful chick questioned loudly.

"I hear you, little colorful chick. I heard your singing as well, and it was precious. There is nothing wrong with your voice, it is just the frequency of your singing. Your voice is very high pitched. We dogs can hear sounds with very high frequencies, but not all beings can hear it. It is only the sensitive ones, those with special abilities. You are a special chick, with special abilities. You should be proud of yourself, so, please, don't be sad. … Your singing is amazing," Mr. Doggy smiled at the small, colorful chick.

"Really, Mr. Doggy? Thank you for your kind words, I needed to hear that!" The colorful chick jumped, encouraged by the realization that it is not mute, but it just had a very special voice.

Singing was the colorful chick's favorite activity. It practiced daily. Even though the rest of the animals in the farm couldn't hear it singing, the colorful chick jumped up on the fence every morning, took up his performing position, and sang his favorite songs.

The days passed simply and in harmony in the farm. The summer came and soon the old couple, the grandfather and grandmother who took care of all the animals on the farm, welcomed their granddaughter, Annie. Her parents brought the little girl to stay with her grandparents in the farm during the summer.

Annie was a young girl, almost six years old. After the summer she was due to start school, where she would face other children for the first time with her social and communicative challenges. Annie had some struggles with expressing herself through language, and she didn't like talking too much. It took her additional effort to express her thoughts. Life in the farm would be good for her; it would give her interesting topics to talk about with her classmates in school.

The little girl was excited about the farm life. From the first day of her arrival, she started to explore the environment around the farmhouse by herself. She went to visit the animals in the yard fearlessly and immediately started to socialize and play with them. The animals all adored her from the first moment they met her, as she was a lovely girl.

Annie woke up early in the morning every day to go with her grandfather to fill the animal's containers with food and fresh water. On one such morning, after finishing the important task of giving food to everyone in the farm, Annie saw the colorful Hummingbird chick. According to its morning routine, it was just preparing to jump up onto the fence and start singing, as always. While the Hummingbird was singing, the lithe girl approached the fence and stood in front of it. When the bird finished its favorite song, Annie applauded it as an audience does a singer on a stage. The girl was amazed by the Hummingbird's stunning voice. It was the first time she

had heard such beautiful, fine singing.

"Oh, you hear me when I sing,
Annie!?" the little Hummingbird
asked curiously.

"Yes, beautiful little bird, I heard
your amazing singing. I like it very
much. You are an amazing singer!"
she said to the Hummingbird with
soft and slow words.

"Thank you, Annie," the Hummingbird answered, and its cheeks
blushed.

"Do you want to be my best friend,
little colorful bird?" Annie asked immediately.

"Yes, Annie, I do! I would be honored
to be your best friend! You must be

a very special girl. Mr. Doggy told me that only beings with special abilities can hear my singing. I will sing you the most beautiful songs every day, Annie, I promise "

From that day, they were inseparable. Every morning, the Hummingbird would sing for Annie, and Annie would enjoy the amazing company of the Hummingbird. They both had special abilities and admired each other unconditionally.

THE END!

BOOKS BY THIS AUTHOR

The Story Of The Red Candy Fish & The Amazing Frog

This is a story about a beautiful friendship between the Red Candy Fish and the Amazing Frog.

The two fellows meet each other in the deepest bottom of the dark ocean, in a moment when they both needed a friend the most. One day, the Amazing Frog invited the Red Candy Fish on his own Secret Island,...

When the Red Candy Fish left the island, the Amazing Frog arranged a great surprise for it, and because of that surprise, the Red Candy Fish and the Amazing Frog became inseparable, forever.

The Story Of The Hungry Boy And The Strawberry Pancakes

Tim's parents are loving and kind in every way, and in return he did everything he could to make them proud. His favourite time of the week, however, was a Sunday morning, when his mother made homemade strawberry jam pancakes and the smell saturated their house. Tim could eat one, two, three portions in one sitting. The problems came, however, when he moved away to become a lawyer. No other food could satisfy Tim, and no other pancakes could compare. He was perpetually hungry, until he met Liza, a beautiful young girl who lived in a picturesque house by a lake, and he found out the secret ingredient of his mom's famous pancakes, which was no other, but love.